SPACE CHASE

Steve Barlow and Steve Skidmore

Illustrated by Santy Gutiérrez

Franklin Watts
First published in Great Britain in 2019 by The Watts Publishing Group

Credits
Series Editor: Adrian Cole
Project Editor: Katie Woolley
Consultant: Jackie Hamley
Designer: Cathryn Gilbert
Illustrations: Santiago Gutiérrez

HB ISBN 978 1 4451 5892 1
PB ISBN 978 1 4451 5891 4
Library ebook ISBN 978 1 4451 5890 7

Printed in China.

FSC
www.fsc.org

MIX
Paper from
responsible sources

FSC® C104740

Franklin Watts
An imprint of
Hachette Children's Group
Part of The Watts Publishing Group
Carmelite House
50 Victoria Embankment
London EC4Y 0DZ

An Hachette UK Company
www.hachette.co.uk

www.franklinwatts.co.uk

THE BADDIES

Lord and
Lady Evil

Dr Y

They want to rule the galaxy.

THE GOODIES

Boo Hoo   Jet   Tip

They want to stop them.

Jet, Tip and Boo Hoo were knocked off their seats.

Jet pointed at the distant ship.

"It's coming back!"

"We have to hide!" moaned Tip.

Boo Hoo pointed to a fancy dress store. "In there!"

Jet groaned.

"It's Butt Hedd! One of the scariest baddies in the whole galaxy!"

"I've followed the space cadets," reported Butt Hedd, "but they're hiding — I can't find them."

Lord Evil's voice crackled from the radio. "I'll send Dr Y. They won't escape his Find-o-Matic detector."

"Fine," agreed Butt Hedd. "What does Dr Y look like?"

"He's got three heads. You can't miss him."

Jet held up a large white lab coat.
"We have everything we need right
here. But we'll have to be quick!"

'Dr Y' stopped at a manhole cover. Jet
pointed at it.

"The cadets are down there."

As they raced back to *Shawn the Ship*,
Jet asked Tip, "Where is Boo Hoo?"
"He's behind us," said Tip.
Jet glanced back. "No, he isn't! What's
he up to?"

28